# BEOWULF

## SILVER EDITION

EDITED BY
ADAPTIVE READER

TRANSLATED BY
FRANCIS BARTON GUMMERE

ISBN: 979-8-8692-6214-1 (paperback)

Ebook: 979-8-8692-6215-8

# INTRODUCTION

Welcome to Adaptive Reader, your portal to the captivating world of literature, tailored to fit your unique reading abilities.

In today's fast-paced and diverse learning environment, we believe in the power of personalized learning experiences. That's where the concept of leveled reading comes in, and why we, at Adaptive Reader, have dedicated ourselves to offering a broad collection of classic novels at various reading levels. Our mission is to make the joy and benefits of reading accessible to everyone.

## THE BENEFITS OF LEVELED TEXTS

So, what exactly is leveled reading? It's an approach that matches students with texts that align with their unique reading abilities. This ensures that every reader is challenged just the right amount - enough to grow, but not so much that they feel overwhelmed or frustrated.

For students, this means you'll engage with texts that stretch your reading skills while keeping the experience enjoyable and manageable. You'll gain confidence as you successfully comprehend each level and feel motivated to explore more challenging texts as your reading skills grow.

For teachers, Adaptive Reader provides a valuable tool to support differentiated instruction. You can assign the same novel to your entire class while ensuring each student reads a version that aligns with their reading level. This allows all students to participate in class discussions and activities, fostering a more inclusive learning environment.

For parents, Adaptive Reader offers a supportive tool to encourage your children's reading journey. As your child progresses through the different levels of a novel, they'll not only enhance their reading skills but also develop a deeper love for literature.

## READING ACROSS MULTIPLE EDITIONS

All of our leveled novels include passage markers that correspond to the same content across every one of our editions. This means that passage '62' in our silver edition contains the same themes and plot elements as passage '62' in our original edition.

For teachers, this means that you can say "let's look at passage 35 together. What is the author trying to tell us here?" and all of your students will be reading the same content — but with vocabulary and syntax that's adapted to their reading level.

Our online reading tool, available at www.adaptivereader.com, gives students and teachers free access to the original text with passage markers. We encourage teachers to include close readings of the original text as part of their coursework, giving all students exposure to the rich original syntax and language of these exceptional authors.

## THE POWER OF LITERATURE

At Adaptive Reader, we are committed to helping everyone experience the power of literature. So whether you're a student diving into a classic novel, a teacher looking for flexible resources, or a parent seeking ways to support your child's literacy, Adaptive Reader is here for you.

We invite you to embark on this exciting literary journey with us. Enjoy the world of stories, characters, and ideas that await you in our collection of leveled novels. Happy reading!

# PRELUDE OF THE FOUNDER OF THE DANISH HOUSE

Long ago, the brave, strong kings of the Danes were praised for their skills with spears.

We have heard stories of their honor

and the victories they achieved. Scyld, a powerful king, would defeat his enemies

and impress his people. He was once a lonely orphan, but fate rewarded him

by making him rich and powerful. Everyone recognized his greatness and gave him gifts.

He became a beloved king.

Scyld had a son, whom heaven sent to help the people who had long needed a leader.

This son, Beowulf, became famous and his actions were well-known in the lands of the Scandians.

It is important for a young prince to treat his father's friends well

by giving them gifts and helping them. Then, those loyal warriors will fight with them in times of war.

They will gain honor and respect from people everywhere through their brave deeds.

When the time came, Scyld went to the safety of God.

His loyal men carried his body to a ship and placed him on it. The ship was strong

and covered in ice as it sailed away, with Scyld resting peacefully on the boat.

The mighty king lay by the mast,

with many treasures brought from distant lands.

I have never seen a ship so finely equipped

with weapons and armor for battle.

On his chest rested a heap of riches

that would float with him far across the sea.

The loyal thanes loaded the ship

with valuable gifts, just as those before had done

when they sent him away as a helpless child.

Above his head, they raised a golden banner,

letting the waves carry him away into the ocean.

Their hearts were heavy, their mood mournful.

No one can truly tell, not a single person,

not even a hero beneath the sky, who carried that cargo!

# BOOK 1

3

Now Beowulf lived in the town of the Scyldings.
He was a beloved leader, and he ruled for a long time
ever since his father had passed
away. Then heirs came,
like proud Healfdene, who held power all his life,
wise and strong, bringing joy to the Scyldings.
Then, one by one, more generations of leaders were born
to the chief of the clan, four in total:
Heorogar, then Hrothgar, then brave Halga;
and I heard that one was queen,
the dear wife of the Heathoscylfing.
Hrothgar was given such glory in battle,
such honor in combat, that all his family
obeyed him willingly, and his group
of young warriors grew large. He had an idea
to have his loyal followers build a great hall,
a grand mead-house, larger and mightier
than anything ever seen before by humans,
and in it, he would give to the old and young

all the gifts that the Lord had granted him,
except for the land and the lives of his men.
I heard that the task was great,
a work that required the effort of many tribes,
to create this gathering place. It was completed quickly,
standing ready there, the grandest of halls.
He named it Heorot, a name known in many lands
for its power and prestige. He generously distributed
rings as gifts during banquets. The hall stood tall,
with wide gables, eagerly waiting
for the burning flames. But it wasn't long
before conflicts once more grew between fathers and sons,
who became filled with anger and envy.
An evil spirit endured the suffering in its dark home,
This spirit heard the joyful sound every day
coming from the hall, where harps played,
and a singer sang tales of the ancient times,
stories of how the Almighty created the Earth,
with beautiful fields surrounded by water,
how the Almighty placed the sun and moon in the sky
to give light to the people living on the land.
He adorned the Earth with plants and trees,
creating life for all living creatures.
The king's men lived happily and celebrated,
enjoying life until something terrible happened.
A fearsome monster named Grendel appeared,
living in the moorlands and marshes,
in a place owned by the giants.
He had been banished there by the Creator.
God sought revenge for the killing of Abel,
who was killed by Cain, a distant ancestor of Grendel.
Cain's descendants, including giants, elves,
and evil spirits, were cursed as a result.
They fought against God, but eventually faced punishment.

# BOOK 11

ONE NIGHT, he went out searching for that proud house to see where the wealthy Danes

had gone to rest after their wild revelry.

Inside, he found the noble warriors sleeping peacefully, unaware of the danger.

The evil creature, fierce and greedy, wasted no time.

He snatched thirty of the warriors from their resting places

and hurried back to his lair, filled with his gruesome trophies. As the day dawned,

Grendel's might became known to the people.

There was moaning and mourning instead of parties,

as the noble leader sat in sorrow, crying over the loss of his warriors.

They had found the cursed monster's trail of blood,

and the sorrow was too much to put up with. The relentless killing happened again the next night.

Grendel wasn't sorry or scared as he kept on killing,

ignoring any sense of right and wrong.

Those who hid were safe from the monster.

It became clear to all that Grendel hated the hall's thane.

Those who stayed away from the hall were spared from the evil creature's clutches.

Grendel ruled without mercy,

wreaking havoc until the once-proud building stood empty

and abandoned for a long time.

For twelve long years, the ruler of the Scyldings carried the burden

of sorrow and countless troubles. The news of these true and terrible events spread among the people.

They sang sad songs about how Grendel, filled with hatred, attacked Hrothgar for many years.

Their fight was never-ending, and Grendel refused to make peace

or accept gold as a bribe.

The wise men had no hope

of ending the conflict.

Grendel would ambush and kill people of all ages, lurking in the dark shadows

and haunting the misty swamps.

No one knew where he came from. He caused constant suffering and terror,

ruling over the golden hall of Heorot during the gloomy nights.

The prince couldn't even approach his own throne or be happy in his hall.

The pain and misery were unbearable for the friend of the Scyldings.

The nobles gathered, looking for advice

on how to stop this terrifying threat. They made offerings

at their pagan altars, begging for an end to their people's suffering.

This was their way, their hope, tied to their beliefs. They did not know

our God, the judge of actions and fearsome Lord, nor did they pay attention to the protection of Heaven. Sadness will come to the person who willingly goes to fiery destruction.

There was no hope or change in sight.

He waits patiently.

But it's good for the person who, after they die, can go to their Lord

and find friendship in the arms of their loving Father.

# BOOK III

8 The son of Healfdene, a wise leader,
was filled with sadness in those days. His people
were burdened with the anguish Grendel caused,
for the monster was a dangerous creature of the night.
One day, a brave warrior who was one of Hygelac's thanes
heard about Grendel's actions. Out of all the Geats,
he was the strongest and bravest.
He decided to get a sturdy ship ready
and set out to find the noble king
who needed help. His loyal friends agreed with
his plan for this journey. They encouraged him
and saw it as a good sign.
With fourteen skilled warriors, he set sail
on the sea. The ship floated smoothly,
guided by the wind, as they carried
their armor and weapons.
As the ship sailed, they spotted
the land's cliffs and hills in the distance.
Finally, they reached their destination.

They had arrived,

and their journey had come to an end.

The people from the Weders clan--the Geats--stepped onto the

shore.

Their boat was secured, and their armor made a clashing sound.

They thanked God for safe passage

across the sea.


From the top of a cliff, a Scylding guard tribe saw them. He was

watching the water

and was surprised to see them carrying shining shields, ready for

battle.

He wondered who they were.

He rode his horse straight to the beach, using his strength to hold

a spear, and spoke to them.

"Who are you, armed men? Why have you brought this powerful

vessel over the ocean to our land?

I am the guard here, protecting the Danish people from any

enemies who may harm us

with their fleet. I have never seen strangers like you so relaxed

and at ease.

You must have missed the treaty with my people before your

arrival.

I've never seen a warrior like that one in the world! He is so

mighty, with such incredible armor.

Please tell me where you come from so that I may know.

Don't walk

around the Danish land like spies. As travelers of the sea, I

advise you

to tell me the name of your country right now."

# BOOK IV

10    THE NOBLEST WARRIOR RESPONDED,

the leader of the warriors spoke.
"We are of the Geatish clan,
friends of King Hygelac. My father
was known far and wide,
a noble prince named Ecgtheow.
He lived many winters,
then passed away as an old man,
but he is still honored
by wise men across the world.
With loyalty and respect,
we come to your lord and king,
Healfdene's son, the protector of his people.
Please tell us where to go!
We have come with an important mission
to the king of the Danes, and I believe
that I must tell the truth. You know
the rumors about a wicked monster
causing terror and death among the Scyldings

during dark, scary nights.
I offer my help to Hrothgar
with great courage and strength
so that the wise and brave can defeat their enemies.
If it is fate that the suffering will end,
the cruel battles will cease,
and peace will return.
Otherwise, Hrothgar will endure
endless days of anguish and sorrow
while that magnificent hall remains empty on the hill!"
The guard on the shore replied,
fearlessly and without hesitation:
"A brave warrior must be able
to wisely choose his words and actions.
I believe your group
comes with good intentions
to serve the master of the Scyldings.
Follow me, armed and prepared,
and I will guide you.
I will assign my men to protect your boat
so that no enemies can approach."
The ship, freshly coated with tar, sat by the shore,
keeping watch and waiting faithfully until it's time
to carry those beloved warriors
across the waters again to the land of the Weders,
to aid and protect them from the horrors of war.
The men prepared to march while the boat remained still,
tied up by ropes and anchored securely,
a wide-bodied vessel. Shining boars glistened
on their helmets, adorned with gold,
sharp and radiant, standing as a guardian
over the warrior. The heroes hurried
until they caught sight of the hall,
with its broad roof and golden glow,

the grandest house on earth, where Hrothgar resided,
its brilliance reaching to far lands.
The courageous soldier pointed to that majestic
fortress, urging Beowulf and his men to go straight there.
Then, he turned his horse and called out:
"It is time for me to leave you. May the Almighty Father
protect you with grace and mercy,
keeping you safe in all you do. I must go towards the sea,
watching out for enemy warriors."

# BOOK V

12 THE BRIGHT PATH led the way for the warriors.

They wore shiny armor and strong helmets. Their swords clinked
as they walked together in a line.

They were tired from their journey across the ocean, but

they pushed through and entered the hall. They placed their
shields and weapons

against the wall and sat down on the benches.

Their armor made loud noises as they moved.

A proud warrior asked them where they came from and who they
were.

"We have come seeking Hrothgar, not as exiles, but as warriors
looking for a courageous leader."

The warrior named Beowulf, a brave warrior from Hygelac's clan,
introduced himself and said he had a message for Hrothgar.

Wulfgar, a respected chief, agreed to take their message
to the king and bring back an answer.

13 Quickly, the messenger hurried to where Hrothgar sat,
surrounded by his loyal followers,

until he stood proudly by the Danish king's side.

Wulfgar, a respected man, addressed his powerful lord,
"Some men from faraway Geatland are here,
after a long, hard journey across the ocean.
The most impressive among them is Beowulf,
accompanied by his brave comrades.
They humbly request the opportunity
to speak with you, my lord.
Please do not dismiss their plea,
but agree to see them, kind Hrothgar!
They are dressed as valiant warriors;
their leader is uno doubt a great hero
who has brought his loyal followers to your kingdom."

# BOOK VI

14  Hrothgar, the king of the Danes, replied:
"I remember Beowulf from his younger days.
His father, Ecgtheow, was a respected man,
and Hrethel, the Geat, married his daughter to him.
Now Beowulf comes here to seek a loyal friend.
I have heard from sailors who brought gifts to the Geats,
thirty of them could barely match Beowulf's strength.
This brave warrior, sent by God,
has come to help us against the monster Grendel.
I will reward him with gold for his bravery.
Go quickly and invite them inside,
the whole group of them, to come before me.
Tell them that they are welcome guests here in Denmark."
Wulfgar went to the door of the hall and shared the message:
"Our king, Hrothgar, welcomes you,
mighty warriors from the east.
You may enter our land in your battle gear,
but leave your shields and weapons outside."
Beowulf and his loyal friends rose to their feet,

leaving some of their men outside to guard their gear.
They followed Wulfgar, who led them inside Heorot's roof.
Beowulf, wearing his gleaming breastplate,
spoke with confidence and strength, standing near the fire.
"Hello, Hrothgar! I am Hygelac's cousin and follower.
I have gained much fame in my youth!
I heard about the terrible things Grendel has been doing.
Sailors tell tales of this great hall, empty and quiet when the sun sets.
So, my loyal followers advised me to seek you out, wise and brave King Hrothgar.
They knew about my strength and courage.
They saw me come back from battles covered in the blood of my enemies,
defeating five of them. I also fought and killed sea monsters
in the dark waves to avenge the suffering of the Weders.
Now, I want to defeat the cruel monster Grendel in a one-on-one fight!
So, I ask you, great King of the Danes, Scyldings' protector, for a favor.
Please don't deny me, Friend-of-the-people, Warriors' shield.
I have traveled far with my loyal followers, and I want to cleanse Heorot, this strong fortress, with them.
I've heard that Grendel doesn't care about weapons, so I won't bring a sword or shield. I will face the
monster with my bare hands and fight for my life.
May the Lord decide my fate.
If I win the fight, I hope to celebrate with my Geatish men in this golden hall."
He will devour my bravest warriors without fear, just like he has done many times before.
You don't have to hide my head if I die in battle,
for he will take it and feast on my blood-covered body

alone in his lonely den, staining his lair in the marsh with my lifeblood.

There is no need to prepare food for me any longer.

If I am taken by death and Hygelac hears of it,

please send him my best armor that protects my chest, the finest war gear,

a precious heirloom from Hrethel and made by Wayland.

Fate will go as it must."

# BOOK VII

17   HROTHGAR SPOKE, the leader of the Scyldings:
    "My friend Beowulf, you have come to help and save us in battle.
    Your father's fight caused a feud
    when he killed Heatholaf of the Wylfings.
    Because of this, his own kin from the Weder tribe
    feared letting him stay and drove him away.
    He sought refuge with our South-Dane people,
    bringing honor to the Scyldings, when I first ruled them.
    I was young and ruled this great kingdom.
    My older brother Heorogar had passed away,
    Healfdene's son, a better man than me.
    I settled the feud with payment to the Wylfings,
    sending them treasures over the ocean.
    He swore oaths to me in return.
    It pains me to tell anyone what grief Grendel has caused me,
    how he has attacked and terrorized Heorot.
    My warriors have been taken by fate, lost to Grendel.
    But God is able to defeat this deadly foe!
    In the drinking hall, they boasted and swore

that they would stay and fight Grendel with their swords.
But the mead-hall was stained with blood at dawn,
the benches covered in gore.
Heroes were lost, brave ones taken by death.
But now, let us feast and speak freely,
brave hero, say what your heart desires."
The Geatish men gathered together.
In the big hall, the strong and brave sat on benches.
A servant came,
holding a beautifully carved cup,
filled with delicious mead. Sometimes musicians played
cheerful songs in Heorot. Heroes celebrated with
plenty of warriors, both from Weder and Dane.

# BOOK VIII

19    UNFERTH, the son of Ecglaf, spoke with envy and challenged Beowulf's achievements.

Unferth asked if Beowulf was the same person
who once competed with Breca
in a daring swimming contest in the open sea.
Unferth said that despite the fierce winter storms and dangerous ocean tides,
Breca had beaten Beowulf.
However, Beowulf argued that he actually had greater strength
and endurance in the water than anyone else.
He dismissed Unferth's drunken claims and boasted of his own skills.

20    We had a conversation when we were young
and made a bet to risk our lives at sea,
though we were just boys at that time.
And we actually did it! We swam with naked swords in our hands,
hoping to protect ourselves from whales.

He couldn't swim far away from me, and I didn't leave him behind either.

We stayed together on the water for five whole nights until the waves separated us.

The churning waves, freezing weather, dark night,

and strong northern wind were all against us.

The angry sea creatures started to appear, but luckily,

my strong linked armor protected me.

I wore a battle suit that covered my chest and was decorated with gold.

The hated enemy grabbed me tightly and dragged me to the bottom,

but I managed to pierce it with my sword.

I defeated the huge sea monster with my brave actions.

# BOOK IX

 I FACED many evil monsters that threatened me.

With my sword, I fought back and gave them what they deserved!

They didn't get to enjoy their prize
or feast on their victims at the bottom of the sea.
Instead, at daybreak, they were defeated by my sword,
lying on the ocean's edge, put to sleep.
Since then, sailors on the boundless sea
are not bothered by those vengeful creatures.
The light from the east, God's beacon, came,
and the waves calmed down,
revealing the tall sea cliffs and windy walls.
Fate often saves a brave warrior
if he isn't doomed!
And so I killed nine sea monsters
with my sword. I've never experienced
a harder battle beneath the sky
or felt more alone than when I was adrift on the vast ocean!
Yet I emerged unharmed from that dangerous encounter,

despite being exhausted from swimming.
The sea carried me to the shores of Finland,
where the rushing waters brought me. I have never heard
of anyone enduring such terrifying sword fights,
such bitter battles. Neither you nor Breca,
either of you brave warriors, have accomplished
such daring feats in war with a bloody sword--
I am not boasting!--
even though you were the ruin of your dear relatives,
your own kin. Hell's curse awaits you,
no matter how clever you may think you are!
For I say truly, son of Ecglaf,
Grendel would not have caused such terrible destruction
in Heorot, attacking your beloved lord,
if your heart was as courageous as your words are loud!
But he thinks he's safe from any battle
with your Danish clan, with no fear
of the Scyldings, the victors of old.
He's bold and ruthless, cold-hearted,
he murders and feasts without fear of
the Spear-Danes' men. But soon,
I'll show him the strength of the Geats,
challenge him to battle to the death.
Let him enjoy his mead for now,
but when the morning light does come,
and the sun will shine bright again."
The Jewel-giver, with joy in his eyes,
heard Beowulf's call.
He knew the Geat would
protect his people and fight with pride.
The liegemen laughed, cheering their heroes with shouts.
Then came Wealhtheow,
the queen of Hrothgar, adorned with gold.
She welcomed the guests and

handed the cup to the heir of the East-Danes,
wishing him joy and happy days,
the beloved ruler of the land.
Hrothgar gladly took the cup in his hand,
enjoying the feast and the mead.
The Helmings' Lady moved through the hall,
offering the cup to each
until it was time to bring Beowulf the mead-filled cup.
She thanked God for him,
a hero to comfort their fears.
He took the cup, his heart strong,
and raised it high, to Wealhtheow's delight.
And Beowulf, ready for battle, replied,
"This was my plan when my warriors and I
set sail in our boat,
that I would fulfill the wishes of your people
completely, or face death in fierce combat,
in the grip of a monster. I am determined
to perform brave deeds as a noble warrior,
or meet my end in this mead-hall."
Beowulf's boastful words pleased the queen.
The noble lady, adorned with gold,
sat beside her husband.
Once again, in the hall, the warriors
celebrated with feasting and powerful words,
the bold revelry of the proud band.
But soon, King Hrothgar sought
rest for the night, knowing that a battle
with the fiend awaited in the festive hall,
when the sun's shine was no longer seen,
and darkness fell over the land,
and ominous shadows appeared
beneath the sky. The warriors stood.
Then, Hrothgar spoke to Beowulf,

welcomed him as the hall's protector, and said,
"Never before have I trusted anyone
with this noble Danish hall,
since I was able to raise sword and shield,
until now, with you.
Take hold of this unmatched house;
remember your glory, declare your might;
stay alert for the enemy! Your desires will be fulfilled
if you face the battle bravely."

# BOOK X

24 Then Hrothgar, the king of the Danes, went with his brave warriors
out of the hall.

He wanted to seek rest with his queen, Wealhtheow.

The King-of-Glory had set a guard against Grendel, the monster.

Everyone heard that there was a hall-defender who protected the
king and watched for the monster.

Beowulf, the prince of the Geats,

had great trust in his strength, power, and in God's mercy.

He took off his iron armor and helmet and gave them to his loyal
follower,

the one with the best sword. He told him to guard the weapons.

Then Beowulf began to boast before he went to bed:

"I am not weaker in battle than Grendel thinks.

But I will not give him death with a sword, even if I have the
chance.

He doesn't have the skill to harm me or cut through my shield.

Tonight, we will fight without swords. If he comes to me,

unarmed and ready for war, let the wisest God decide who will
win."

Then Beowulf lay down, resting his head on his pillow.

The brave sailors also settled on their beds in the hall. None of them knew

that they would not return to their loved ones and the land they cherished.

They knew that many warriors who sat in the banquet-hall had been taken

by death in battle. But they hoped for comfort and help,

may it be given to the people of the Weder tribe, seeking their fortunes in war.

The mighty Master controlled the outcome,

defeating all enemies through one person's strength.

It is said that the greatest God above mankind

has always held this power! In the pale night,

the shadowy figure walked, while warriors slept,

their duty to protect the hall's roofed peaks--

except for one. Everyone knew

that the ghostly intruder couldn't force him

into death against God's will;

so he stayed awake, prepared, with the anger of a warrior,

bravely waiting for the battle's end.

# BOOK XI

26 FROM THE MARSHY LAND, near misty rocks,

Grendel approached with anger from God. The monster had a plan

to attack the people in their grand house.

He wandered beneath the sky until he saw the magnificent wine palace,

shining with beautiful decorations. This wasn't

the first time Grendel had come to Hrothgar's home,

but he had never encountered such brave heroes and loyal warriors before.

He quickly approached the house,

breaking through the strong door, fueled by his fury.

As he entered, he stomped aggressively across the well-made floor,

his eyes flashing like terrifying flames.

Inside the hall, he spotted the sleeping hero-band,

Hrothgar's relatives and loyal followers.

Grendel laughed with joy because he planned to kill

each and every one of them before dawn, as he longed for a gruesome feast.

However, fate had decreed that he wouldn't be able to harm any more humans after that night.

Hygelac's relative, who was watching closely, eagerly observed
how Grendel would fare in his violent attack.

But the monster had no intentions of stopping.

He immediately grabbed the first sleeping warrior he could find
and tore him apart.

He gnawed on the bones, drank the blood,
and devoured the body piece by piece until there was nothing left,
not even the hands and feet.

Then, Grendel continued on his path.

The mighty hero grabbed the monster's hand,
searched for the enemy with the wicked claw,
found him lying there then boldly held on,
ready to fight back, propped on his arm.

The evil creature soon realized
he had never encountered in this world
someone with a stronger grip than he.

He felt the fear deep down, his heart filled with sorrow,
unable to escape!

He wanted to flee, to find safety in his den,
the lair of demons—no longer able
to do what he had done in days past.

Then the brave Beowulf, loyal to Hygelac,
remembered his evening boast: he stood up,
firmly grasped his foe until its fingers cracked.

The monster tried to escape, but the warrior pursued.

If he could, the creature meant to break free,
fly far away to the marshes—he knew
the strength of this Beowulf's fingers, the grip of the fierce one.

The harmful monster had caused enough chaos in Heorot!

The room was filled with noise, the Danes lost
their castle, their kinsmen, their brave warriors,
all the lords, and even their ale. Both
ferocious fighters were furious—the house echoed.
It was a marvel how the wine hall stood strong,
resisting the force of their fight; the beautiful house
didn't collapse, held together tightly
by its cleverly crafted iron bands,
even though many a mead-bench crashed
from the wall—I've been told—
where the fierce foes wrestled.
The wisest Scyldings had believed
that no man in existence would ever be able
to break apart that noble house.
He tried to destroy it with his smarts,
but it was protected from fire's embrace.
The noise intensified once again.
The people of Denmark in the north
were filled with fear and panic
as they heard the wailing from the wall.
The enemy of God sang his horrifying song,
crying out in pain as a captive of hell.
No one could free themselves from Beowulf's tight grip,
not even the strongest among us.

# BOOK XII

29 THE WARRIORS KNEW they couldn't let the dangerous stranger live.

They believed his existence brought no benefit to anyone on Earth,

so they were determined to protect their lord, Beowulf.

Each earl wielded their ancestral swords,

hoping to defend their praised prince if they had the power.

But as they approached the foe, they soon realized that no blade,

no matter how sharp or well-crafted,

could harm the hideous fiend.

He was protected by spells and immune to their weapons.

However, they knew that his end would come on that very day.

His soul would wander off to the domain of fiends.

This fiend, who had caused harm and was hated by God,

had now met his match. The courageous relative of Hygelac

held him tightly, and both despised each other.

The outlaw suffered a fatal injury,

with a mighty wound on his shoulder, cracked muscles, and broken bones.

Beowulf received the glory,

while Grendel retreated to his dark and foul den in the moor,
knowing that this was the end of his life on Earth.
This bloody battle brought a blessing to all the Danes.
The foreign stranger had saved Hrothgar's hall from destruction
and had cleansed it once again.
Beowulf was satisfied with his victory.
He proved his bravery and brought honor to the Danish people
from the East.
The courageous Geat ended their troubles
and sadness by fighting the battles and hardships they had long
endured.
This was proven when he defeated Grendel
and freed the Danes from the monster's grip,
releasing its arm and shoulder from his powerful hand
within the hall.

# BOOK XIII

31 MANY PEOPLE GATHERED in the morning, as others have told me.

The warriors came from near and far

to see the hall and see the remains of the traitor.

The enemy's defeat did not bother anyone who saw

how the tired, banished monster stumbled away to die

in his demonic lake.

The waves were bloody and boiling, the tides were rough and swirling,

with the heat of sword-blood from the doomed one who would die in his dark den,

forsaking his heathen soul.

The old chieftains rode home with joy, and the brave warriors

on their white horses returned from the lake.

They praised Beowulf's glory and agreed

that there was no bigger hero in all the lands,

from north to south and from sea to sea.

They respected and admired their beloved lord,

gracious Hrothgar, for he was a good king.

Sometimes, the warriors raced with their gray horses on the open road.

And sometimes, one of the king's loyal followers, who was skilled in storytelling,

recited old legends and songs in well-crafted verses.

He cleverly sang about Beowulf's quest and added a great tale to his song.

Long ago, a warrior told a tale

of a man named Sigemund's heroic deeds.

It was a strange story, he told of

the wanderings and struggles of the Waelsing,

which were unknown to other tribes,

except for Fitela, his nephew,

whom he trusted with his secrets.

They fought side by side in war,

slaying many monstrous creatures.

When Sigemund died, he was given great praise,

for he killed a dragon that guarded a treasure hoard,

bravely facing the terrifying quest alone,

without Fitela by his side.

With a powerful strike of his sword,

he pierced the dragon's heart,

ending its life and spilling its blood.

By this daring act, Sigemund became

the owner of the treasure,

taking the gold and loading it onto a ship.

He was praised by all as the greatest hero,

earning a reputation among all people

for his courageous deeds, unlike the failed hero, Heremod,

who lost his strength and courage in battle.

Heremod was banished and left to face monsters,

betrayed by sorrow and burdened with care.

Many wise men mourned for the days

when they had hoped for Hermod's help and protection.

Many people believed that the king's son would be a great ruler
and protect his people, the treasure, and the land of the heroes,
the Scyldings' home.

However, his cousin, who was kinder to everyone, seemed to be
favored instead of the son.

The roads were now busy with people rushing to the grand hall
to witness something amazing.

The king, adorned with jewels and respected by all, made
his way
from the bridal chamber to the great hall,
accompanied by the queen and her group of young women.

# BOOK XIV

34    Hrothgar spoke, walked into the hall,
stood by the steps, and looked up at the tall roof
that was decorated with gold and Grendel's arm.
"I quickly thank the God
for what I see! I have endured many sorrows
from Grendel, but God continues
to perform miracles, the Guardian of Glory.
I no longer have to wait
for help with the troubles that burdened me
for so long. This noble house, stained with sword-blood,
had meant sorrow to all wise men,
who had no hope of ever stopping
our enemies and these evil spirits
from causing destruction in our hall. But now,
by the power of the Almighty, this hero
has done something with his wisdom and bravery
that none of us could have done before.
Truly, the woman who gave birth to this warrior
can proudly say, if she still lives,

that the God of the ages was kind to her
when her child was born. Now, Beowulf,
I will love you dearly like my own son,
the best among heroes. Always preserve
this new kinship, and you will never lack
for wealth of the world that I possess!
I have rewarded others with my precious treasure
for less, men who were weaker in battle. But you
have now accomplished such deeds that your fame
will endure throughout the ages. Just as he has always done,
may the Almighty continue to reward you!"
Beowulf, son of Ecgtheow, spoke:
"We willingly fought this war,
this battle, and fearlessly faced
the strength of the enemy. I also wish
that you had seen him yourself, when
The mighty monster stumbled in his armor!
Quickly, I thought, I would grip him tightly
on his deathbed, so he could take his last breath
in my hand's grasp. But he managed to escape.
I could not stop him--it was the will of the Creator--
from fleeing, though I held the life-destroyer firmly.
He was too strong and ruthless in his running!
But as he fled, he left behind his hand,
arm, and shoulder as a pledge,
unable to get any help in return.
Now, that hated fiend no longer lives.
He is bound tightly by sorrow and anguish,
held captive in its bonds,
as the Mighty Maker decides his awful fate."
The son of Ecglaf became quieter
when boasting about his battle,
as all the noble warriors saw
the enemy's fingers on the high roof,

with nails as strong as steel,
like a heathen's "hand-spear,"
a strange and dangerous claw. They realized
that no brave blade could harm him,
no matter how sharp, or cut off
that bloodied arm from its wicked owner.

# BOOK XV



There was a rush of activity in Heorot,
as hands prepared the hall for a party.
People came to clean and decorate,
hanging beautiful cloths on the walls
to delight all who looked upon them.
Though the building was strong,
it had been damaged by Grendel,
its hinges broken, its walls tested.
But the roof remained intact,
providing a safe haven for those inside.
The time came for Healfdene's son to enter,
the king himself ready to feast.
I have never seen a grander gathering,
with humble guests surrounding the generous lord.
The special guests took their places at the table,
joyfully receiving their mead-cups.
Hrothgar and Hrothulf sat among their cousins
as Heorot filled with laughter and friendship.
The Scyldings had never before put up with evil,

and they offered Beowulf tokens of their thanks.
Healfdene's son gave Beowulf
a splendid banner, crafted of gold,
and a sword that many admired.
Beowulf raised his cup in the hall,
thankful for these valuable gifts.
He felt proud to be among these brave warriors.
Not many heroes had been given such splendid gifts!
A golden ridge ran along the top of the helmet
to protect his head from sharp attacks.
Eight horses with carved headgear were led into the hall.
One horse stood out with a shining saddle and jeweled deco-
rations.
It belonged to the great king who always fought with valor.
Beowulf was never defeated in battle.
He was given the horses and weapons.
The mighty prince rewarded him for his hard fight
with valuable treasures that everyone loved.

# BOOK XVI

38 AND THE LORD OF CHIEFS, to each person who arrived
with Beowulf on the vast ocean waves,
gave a special gift at the feast,
a valuable treasure of gold,
in honor of the one whom Grendel
had killed.
But the wisest God had changed his fate,
protecting the hero.
The Creator ruled over humanity,
both then and now.
Therefore, it is always best
to be wise and think ahead.
For there are many joys and sorrows
in store for those who live in this world
through days of war.
Then songs and music filled the air
in the presence of Healfdene's warrior chief,
and the harpist played a heroic tune,
awakening joy in the hall

as Hrothgar's poet shared
the story of the sudden attack on Finn's sons.
Healfdene's hero, Hnaef the Scylding,
was destined to fall in battle with the Frisians.
Hildeburh did not hold her enemies' honor in high regard.
Both her child and brother,
innocent and dear to her,
were casualties of war, victims
of spears, and it brought great sadness.
It was no one wonder why Hoc's daughter
grieved at dawn when she saw,
under the sky, her loved ones lying dead,
those she cared for most in the world.
Finn's loyal followers were also swept away by war,
and only a few remained.
He could no longer speak
or fight against Hengest,
and he couldn't save the survivors
by using his own army.
He proposed a peace agreement instead:
The Danes were promised another home,
a grand hall and a seat of honor,
and they would have half the power
in the Frisian land as well.
Folcwald's son would honor the Danes
and favor Hengest's people with rings,
just as he intended to honor his Frisian kin
with precious treasures and gold.
They made the pact of peace
on both sides, with firm promises.
Finn, with an oath and on his honor,
promised openly to govern the remaining Danes,
with the help of wise advisors,
so that none of the guests would break the treaty

with words or actions, or feel compelled
to follow their fee-giver's killer as lordless men.
If a Frisian were to provoke them with enemy taunts,
his fate would be sealed by the sword.
Oaths were exchanged, and ancient gold
was shared from a treasure hoard.
The brave Scylding, the best warrior, lay on his funeral pyre.
All could see on the pyre
the bloodstained shirt, the golden boar crest,
and many noble warriors slain by the sword.
At Hnaef's funeral pyre, as commanded by Hildeburh,
the child born of her own body was placed on burning brands,
his bones would burn side by side with his uncle's.
The woman wept in sorrowful songs,
and her wailing filled the air.
Then the highest flames reached the sky,
the fiercest of funeral fires,
roaring over the mound.
Heads dissolved, wounds burst open,
and blood poured out.
40  The fire burned and took away
the lives of those who survived the battle.
It consumed them, leaving no one left from either group.
Their best people were gone.

# BOOK XVII

41  THE HEROES HURRIED BACK to their homeland in the Frisian land.

They found houses and a high fortress.

Hengest, still staying with Finn, remained faithful to their agreement.

However, he missed his home but couldn't sail his ship
because the fierce waves and icy winter held them back.
Another year went by, the sun shining in the sky,
as they patiently awaited the right season.
Finally, the harsh winter passed, and the earth looked beautiful.
The traveler, eager to leave, also thought about
taking revenge and facing the Frisians' sons.
Unfortunately, he couldn't escape fate.
Hun stabbed him with the famous sword called "Lafing."
Finn, too, met his end when Guthlaf and Oslaf attacked him
in his own home.
They were avenging their own sorrows from their sea journey.
Finn's spirit couldn't bear the weight of guilt. The fortress was soaked
with enemies' blood, and Finn, the king, was killed.

The queen was taken captive, and the Scylding warriors

took all of Finn's treasures and brought them to their ship.

They also led the gentle wife back to her homeland.

And that concludes the story.

 Then the poet sang his song.

The revelers were happy and the joyful feeling filled the room.

The servers brought wine from their amazing vats.

Wealhtheow, the queen, emerged wearing a golden crown,

and approached the uncle and nephew who sat together.

They were loyal and friendly towards each other.

Unferth, the one who spoke on behalf of the Scylding lord, sat at
his feet.

People trusted in his bravery, even though his relatives

had doubts about his skills in sword fighting.

The queen of the Scyldings spoke up and said,

"My king and lord, take a drink from this cup. Enjoy yourself,

the golden friend of men.

Speak kindly to the Geats, as one should. Be grateful

for the gifts you have received, whether near or far.

People say to me that you wish for this hero to become your son.

Take pleasure in your bright jewel-hall, Heorot, while you
still can.

Be generous with your gifts and leave your people

and kingdom to your kin when you face your fate.

I believe my Hrothulf will rule and take care of our young ones
with honor

if you give up your role as the prince of the Scyldings.

I trust that he will appreciate our children

and repay them for all the support and kindness

we have given him throughout his childhood."

Then she turned to the seat where her sons, Hrethric and
Hrothmund,

sat with the young heroes.

Beowulf, the brave Geat, also sat among them as a brother.

# BOOK XVIII

43   SHE HANDED HIM A CUP, greeted him kindly, and spoke with gentle words.

> She offered him two beautiful arm-jewels made of gold,
> a jeweled breastplate, rings, and the finest collars I had ever seen.
> I had never heard of a more magnificent treasure in all the world.
> It was a gem fit for heroes, like the legendary Brisings' treasure
> that Hama once brought to his splendid city.
> It was a jewel-filled chest. Hama obtained it and escaped the hatred of Eormenric.
> He chose eternal help over Eormenric's hate.
> On his last raid, Hygelac, the Geat and grandson of Swerting,
> took this ring with him to defend his spoils and
> protect the stolen goods under his banner of war.
> But fate overwhelmed him, as he faced dangers in his daring feud with the Frisians.
> The king's body fell into the hands of the Franks
> along with his breastplate and the beautiful ring.
> Weaker warriors took the spoils from the lord of the Geats
> after a fierce battle and claimed victory.

A loud noise now filled the hall.

Wealhtheow spoke among the warriors and said,

"Enjoy this precious jewel in your joyful youth, beloved Beowulf.

Wear this armor, a royal treasure, and grow rich. Preserve your strength

and show kindness to these young warriors.

Let me offer my gratitude for your brave deeds

that have made you famous among people near and far,

as far-reaching as the waves of the ocean.

May you thrive in the journey of life, O prince!

I pray that you acquire great wealth.

And to my son, I hope you will gain great honor and glory just like him.

Everyone was helpful to each other, loyal to their leader.

The warriors were happy and followed the rules. They listened and obeyed.

Then Wealhtheow went back to her seat.

It was the best feast. They drank wine and didn't care what would happen in the future.

Hrothgar would go home and rest.

The room was protected by soldiers, just like before.

They cleared the benches and made beds. One person who drank too much fell asleep in the hall.

They put their shields and weapons next to them on the benches.

Everyone had a helmet, spear, and armor.

It was their tradition to always be ready for battle, whether at home or out fighting.

They were loyal followers of their king.

# BOOK XIX

45 THEN THEY FELL ASLEEP. One by one, they sadly took their rest for the evening.

This had happened many times before,
when Grendel haunted the golden hall and caused trouble
until his end, bringing a rampage of death for his sins.
It was witnessed and told how an avenger survived the monster,
and this news spread far and wide.
After that fierce battle, Grendel's mother, a monstrous woman, mourned her sadness.
She was destined to live in the dreary waters, in the cold sea,
because her ancestor Cain had killed his own brother with a sword.
He became an outlaw, marked with murder,
fleeing from society and dwelling in the wilderness.
From him came dreadful ghosts like Grendel,
who found a warrior waiting for him in the great hall of Heorot.
The two of them fiercely fought each other.
But the man remembered the great power that God had given him.

He trusted in his Maker's mercy for comfort and help.

With that trust, he defeated the enemy,

slaying the fiend who fled in misery to the land of death, the enemy of mankind.

Now his mother, gloomy and fierce, sought revenge for her son's death.

Grendel's mother came to Heorot, where the Danes were sleeping in their helmets.

The old troubles returned as soon as she burst into the hall.

However, her terror was not as great as that of a woman in war

compared to the might of armed men when a well-made sword, stained with blood, pierced a war helmet.

In the hall, swords were drawn, shields firmly held,

and helmets and armor ignored by those who were gripped with fear.

The creature hurried, wanting to escape and save her life

after the warriors saw her.

She managed to grab just one brave warrior,

a favorite of Hrothgar and a trusted vassal,

whom she killed on his bed.

Beowulf was not there; he had been given a separate place to stay

with his reward of gold for his bravery.

Chaos filled Heorot as everyone saw the blood-stained hand she carried with her.

Sorrow and grief filled the homes as Danish and Geatish families

were destined to lose their loved ones.

The wise old king, who had been through so much, was heartbroken

when he learned that his noble warrior was no longer alive.

They quickly brought Beowulf to his chamber, the fearless victor.

As morning arrived, the noble hero, accompanied by his warriors,

entered the king's presence, eager to hear if the Ruler of All

would address this tale of trouble and sorrow.

The famous warrior walked across the floor,
the sound echoing throughout the hall,
and approached the wise old king,
lord of the Ingwines, asking if the night had passed without incident.

# BOOK XX



King Hrothgar spoke, the leader of the Scyldings, and said:
"Do not ask about joy! Pain has returned
to our Danish people. Aeschere is dead,
the older brother of Yrmenlaf,
my wise advisor and support in our meetings,
my loyal companion in times of battle.
We defended our heads and fought warriors,
and now every noble should mourn Aeschere's loss!
But here, in Heorot, someone has killed him,
a wandering evil spirit. I do not know where she went,
proud of her prey and
satisfied with her kill. She avenged the feud
that happened last night, relentlessly.
You bravely killed Grendel, despite
all the harm he caused to my loyal warriors. Now another
comes, fierce and cruel, to avenge her kin,
seeking bloodshed and revenge.
Many chiefs will think, whoever
grieves for that lord of rings,

this is the most heartbreaking sorrow. The hand now lies still
that was willing to grant every wish.
People of this land and my loyal subjects,
who live near those parts, have told me
that they have sometimes seen a pair of
mighty wanderers haunting the moorland,
mysterious spirits: one of them seemed,
as far as my people could tell,
to be a woman; and the other, cursed,
was in the form of a man,
although larger than any human.
They called him Grendel in the old days,
the people of this land; they did not know his father,
nor any offspring born to him
from deceitful spirits. Their home remains untouched.
They haunt the cliffs where wolves live,
scary paths and windy headlands.
A stream flows from the mountains to the rocks,
underground. Not far away, the lake expands,
covered by frosty trees that create shadows.
At night, a strange thing can be seen,
fire on the water. No human was wise enough
to explore those depths! Even if a scared deer,
chased by dogs, was forced to seek refuge in this lake,
it would rather give up its life at the edge
than take the risk of diving in. It's not a happy place!
The waves crash and reach the sky
when the winds stir up evil storms,
and the air grows dark,
and the sky cries. Now, once again,
you are the only one who can help! You don't know
the terrifying land, where you will find
that sinful creature. Go if you dare!

If you succeed in this fight,

I will reward you with even more piles of ancient treasure,

just like I did before,

with beautiful gold, if you come back victorious."

# BOOK XXI

49   Beowulf, son of Ecgtheow, spoke:
"Don't be sad, wise one! It is better for us
to avenge our friends than to mourn them in vain.
Each one of us must face our end
in this world's ways, so let those who can
seek their glory before death! When his time comes,
that is the greatest fate for a warrior.
Now, rise up, protector of the kingdom!
Let us ride soon and follow the trail
of Grendel's mother. No hiding place
will be safe from us. She can run wherever she wants,
whether it be open fields or forests or mountains,
or even the depths of the sea. It doesn't matter!
But for now, you must be patient,
as I believe you will, with every trouble you face."
The old king leaped up and thanked God,
the mighty Lord, for the brave words of the man.
For Hrothgar, a strong, swift horse was saddled,
a horse with a mane like the waves. The wise king

rode proudly, with his men armed and ready,
following in force. The footprints led them
through the woods and across the plains,
where she had passed and stomped
in the dark marshes. The fallen warrior,
the bravest and best, was carried by her,
the one who ruled the king's home alongside Hrothgar.
Beowulf, born a noble prince, continued on,
scaling steep cliffs and narrow paths,
squeezing through tight passages and unknown trails,
along sheer cliffs and the homes of dangerous creatures.
He led the way, accompanied by a few
of the wisest men who could scout the route,
until he suddenly found himself facing
a forested hill looming over a gray rock,
a woeful forest, with blood-stained waves below.
The Danish men, as well as the Scyldings,
felt deep sadness in their hearts, as it was hard to look at for many of the heroes.

It was a sad time for the brave men when they found
Aeschere's head by the river's edge.
The waves were full, the warriors saw,
Hot with blood. But their horn sang
A bold battle song. The group sat down,
And watched strange worm-like creatures on the water,
Sea-dragons and monsters that made deep sounds,
And sea-snakes on the shores.
They often come at dawn to search ruthlessly
On the waves for their prey.
These creatures swam away, scared and fierce,
When they heard the sound of the war horn.
Then the protector of Geats shot an arrow
From his bow, and it hit one monster's heart,
Making it weaker in the water.

With sharp spears like boar's tusks,
They fought hard and killed the monster,
Dragging it onto the shore.
The warriors looked at the terrifying creature.
Then Beowulf put on his strong armor,
Not afraid of losing his life.
His broad, brightly colored breastplate,
Hand-woven, protecting him in the water.
No enemy could harm his heart.
His white helmet, designed to dive into deep waters,
Was made with chains and decorated with gold,
Just like in the old days
It was beautifully crafted with images of boars.
Beowulf received great help when he needed it.
The sword was called "Hrunting," a powerful weapon
with a long history.
Its blade was made of strong iron and coated with poison.
It was known for its abilities in battle and never failed the hero
who wielded it on dangerous missions.
This sword had a reputation for accomplishing daring tasks.
However, Ecglaf's son didn't remember the speech
its previous owner had made when he was drunk with wine.
He lent the sword to Beowulf, but never had the courage to risk
his life underwater.
This decision cost him his reputation and the respect of others.
But Beowulf, who now wielded the sword, was prepared for the
challenging fight ahead.

# BOOK XXII



Beowulf spoke, brave son of Ecgtheow:
"Listen, noble child of Healfdene,
trusted friend of men. As I start this journey,
remember what was once said:
If I were to lose my life in your cause,
promise to stand by me, even in my father's place.
Protect my group of loyal warriors
if we are attacked in battle.
And please send the generous gifts
you gave me, beloved Hrothgar, to Hygelac!
When he sees the gold from Geatland's king,
when he sees the treasure,
may he know that I made a famous friend,
and that I delighted in your generosity.
And let Unferth, the respected warrior,
lift this amazing sword,
passed down through generations, its edge sharp.
With my own sword, Hrunting, I will seek glory,
or face death."

After saying these words, the brave lord from the land of the Weder-Geats

hurriedly went on his way without waiting for an answer.

The ocean's waves closed over the hero,

and he spent a long time beneath the sea before he felt the ocean floor.

Then the monster, Grendel's mother, who had ruled the underwater land for a hundred years and hungered for swords,

realized that a visitor from above, a man, was invading her domain.

She reached out with her gruesome claws, trying to grab him,

but she could not harm his strong body.

His breastplate protected him as she tried to break his armor,

his linked chainmail blocked her disgusting hand.

When she reached the ocean floor,

the sea-wolf carried the lord of rings to her haunted lair.

As he bravely fought, though his strength remained,

he tried to defend himself against the terrifying monsters

that surrounded him; many sea creatures

tried to tear his armor with their sharp tusks,

swarming around the stranger. But soon he realized

that he was now inside a hall, though he didn't know which one,

where the water couldn't harm him,

and the roof protected him from their fangs.

He saw the flickering light of a fire,

the beams shining brightly.

Then the warrior noticed the monstrous woman,

the fearsome creature. Without hesitation,

he swung his sword, delivering a powerful blow.

The blade struck her head with a resounding song of war.

But the warrior discovered that the sword's edge,

which had faithfully served him before,

now failed to harm his opponent's heart.

Although it had seen countless battles and split helmets,

it couldn't pierce the beast's hide. This was the first time
this shining blade failed in its glory.
However, the noble warrior remained steadfast,
undaunted in his bravery, the relative of Hygelac.
He discarded the ornate and decorated sword,
angrily throwing it aside. It lay on the ground,
sharp and rigid. He trusted in his own strength,
the mighty grip of his hand. This is what a man should do
when seeking to achieve everlasting fame in war,
without fearing for his life!
Seized by the shoulder, he didn't hesitate to engage
Grendel's mother, the war-princess.
Filled with anger, he forcefully flung his deadly foe,
causing her to fall to the ground.
But she swiftly retaliated,
grabbing him with her monstrous hands and struggling
with him.
The warrior grew weak and stumbled,
the strong fighter fell to the ground.
She attacked the guest in the hall,
wielding her short sword, seeking revenge
for her only child. But his shoulder was protected
by strong armor, saving him from death,
shielding him from the sharp blade.
The son of Ecgtheow would have died,
buried in the earth, if not for his armor
and the power of God, the wise Creator,
who granted him victory over his enemy.
With God's help, the brave warrior rose again.

# BOOK XXIII

55  IN THE MIDST of the battle, he noticed a powerful sword,
an ancient weapon of the Eotens, with a proven edge,
a treasured heirloom of warriors, unmatched in its strength,
although it was heavier than what most men could handle.
It was expertly crafted by the giants, sharp and ready.
The leader of the Scyldings grabbed the sword by its chain-hilt.
Bold and fearless, he swung the sword,
not caring for his own life, and struck with great anger,
gripping her neck tightly, breaking her bone-rings.
The blade pierced through the doomed creature's flesh, and she
fell to the floor.
The sword was covered in blood, and he felt a sense of satis-
faction.
Suddenly, the room was filled with a bright light,
as if a clear candle from the sky was shining down.
He scanned the hall and approached the wall,
raising his weapon high with eagerness and anger,
determined to use this sword effectively.
He wanted to seek revenge on Grendel,

for the terrible attacks he had made on the people of Western-
Danes.

Grendel had repeatedly invaded Hrothgar's hall,

killing and devouring fifteen warriors in their sleep,

and carrying away just as many as his horrifying prey.

The prince's anger was justified! Now, lying prone on the floor,

he saw Grendel also dead, exhausted from the battle,

stripped of life, having suffered greatly

at the hands of Heorot's warriors. Grendel's body

sprang far away when the fatal sword-strike

severed its head. Soon after, the wise companions saw the
outcome.

The wise men who waited with Hrothgar watched the turbulent
flood

as the waters grew murky and stained with blood.

The old men, with their hoary hair, spoke of the hero

who they thought would not return in triumph to their great
king.

Many believed that the sea woman had claimed his life.

As the ninth hour came, the noble Scyldings left the headland
and went back home.

But the Geats remained, staring at the waves, feeling sick and
hoping to see their beloved lord once more.

Suddenly, that sword, soaked in battle blood, began to weaken
and shrink,

like ice melting when the Father of Frost releases his frozen
chains.

He controls all seasons and times--the true God!

The Geatish leader took only the head of the slain fiend and the
hilt adorned with jewels;

the blade had melted away, burnt by the hot blood and poisoned
by the wicked spirit

that had perished inside it.

Soon, the victorious hero, who had witnessed the death of demons in battle,

began to swim and rise from the water. The clashed waves were now calm, with no trace of the dreadful creature that

had lost her life in this fading world.

He swam to the shore, filled with strength and joy, carrying the spoils of his brave deeds.

The chosen comrades of the

cheerful chief greeted him and thanked God for his safe return.

They were relieved and happy to see him safe again.

Quickly, they helped him remove his helmet and armor.

The water in the lake was now calm and peaceful, stained with the blood of the battle.

They walked back along the familiar paths, feeling joyful and brave.

The brave men carried Grendel's head from the cliff by the sea, which was a difficult task that required

four strong warriors.

With courage, fourteen Geats marched towards the palace, fearless of their enemies,

with their mighty leader among them.

The respected leader, known for his bravery, fearlessly entered the hall and greeted Hrothgar.

They brought Grendel's head into the hall by its hair, where the people were drinking,

astonishing both the clan and the queen.

Everyone in the hall looked in awe at the monstrous head.

# BOOK XXIV

58   Beowulf spoke, son of Ecgtheow:

"Look, we have brought you this treasure from the sea,
a symbol of glory that you see here.
I did not escape with my life easily!
I fought underwater with great effort,
and I would have been defeated without the Lord's protection.
Hrunting, a good weapon, did not work for me in battle;
but the Lord granted me a sword
to find on the wall, hanging in splendor.
He often helps those who have no friends!
With that sword, I fought the guardians of the house,
and it burned brightly when covered in blood and sweat.
I brought back the handle from my enemies.
I avenged the Danish people by killing the fiends,
as was necessary and just.
Now, I command that you can sleep safely in Heorot,
with your soldiers and all your people,
young and old. Lord of the Scyldings, you have no reason to fear,

any harm to your noble warriors from that side as you did
before!"
Then the golden hilt, made by giants, was placed in the hand
of the elderly hero, as an honored possession,
after the defeat of the devils and the death of the Danish lord.
It was a masterpiece created by skilled craftsmen,
and now the world was rid of the fierce enemy,
a murderer marked with evil, and also his mother.
Now, the hilt belonged to the king of the people.
The mighty oceans hold treasures,
scattered gold on Scandia's shores.
Hrothgar looked at the ancient hilt,
a relic of a distant battle.
When the giants' hearts had grown apart from God,
the Ruler punished them with floods.
In the watery waste, their lives ended.
Glowing gold runes told
the tale of the sword, made where serpents did dwell,
the finest blade of long ago days,
with a well-wound hilt.
The wise one spoke, Healfdene's son,
and silence fell as he said:
"May those who follow truth
bring honor to their people,
a longtime keeper of the land such as you,
a noble breed.
Let your fame be spread far and wide,
Beowulf, my friend, due to your strength,
the wisdom that guides you and helps you lead
your homeland.
My love is yours,
a support for you in times ahead,
for your people and their future.
They will treasure your protection for all time.

But Heremod, Ecgwela's son, was not the same,
for he had no grace but rather a grim demeanor,
bringing death to Danishmen in battle.
He slew his comrades as
a haughty chieftain.
Though gifted by the Creator's strength,
with power and glory shining bright,
his mind was filled with bloodlust.
His treasure of riches grew, but he did not share
with the Danes as he should have done;
he endured the burden of struggle and the weight of sorrow,
a long-lasting feud with his own people. Learn from this!
Seek virtue! This verse is for you,
wise one with many winters behind you. It is astonishing
how Almighty God grants wisdom to humankind
through the strength of His spirit,
providing honor and status. He controls all things.
At times, He allows the hero of noble birth
to do well with courage and joy,
giving him a secure kingdom,
the safety of his people as their rightful ruler.
He grants him power over vast lands,
a grand empire that some consider limitless.
In this wealth and success, he is shielded from harm,
immune to illness and the effects of aging;
no worries bother his soul. No enemies threaten him with
swords.
He commands the world to do as he says,
facing no hardship until within him,
stubborn pride begins to grow.
The guardian of his spirit sleeps.
Sleep tightly holds him, as the killer draws near,
silently shooting arrows from his bow!

# BOOK XXV

61  HIS HEART GETS HURT when he wears armor and no shelter protects him

> from the evil fiend. He feels like what he had is not enough.
> He doesn't give out golden rings because he is greedy and mean.
> He forgets the things God sent him, like wealth and fame.
> But someday, his body will get weak and he will die.
> Then, someone else will take his place and enjoy the treasures.
> Beowulf, don't have these bad thoughts.
> Choose the better path and be humble. Your strength won't last forever.
> Sickness, swords, fire, water, blades, and old age will weaken you.
> Death will come for you, hero. I ruled the Ring-Danes for a hundred years
> and protected them from enemies.
> But then, Grendel attacked and caused me so much sorrow.
> I am thankful to God for letting me live longer.

62  I want to see this head, chopped and bloody,
> after a long battle, with my own eyes!

Go sit at the table now. Enjoy the feast,
worthy warrior! A treasure of wealth
will be divided between us at dawn!"
The Geats' lord was happy and quickly
went to his seat, as the wise man instructed.
Once again, a noble banquet was prepared
for the famous warriors in the hall.
The night grew dark as the drinking continued.
The brave ones rose:
the elderly leader wanted to rest,
the aged Scylding and the eager Geat,
a strong shield-fighter, longed for sleep.
A weary warrior-guest from afar
was summoned by a hall-thane,
who, in the custom of olden days,
attended to the needs of wandering warriors.
So the brave-hearted man slumbered. The hall stood
grand and decorated where the guest slept
until a black raven predicted
the joyous light of dawn. The warriors hurried,
all nobles eager to return home;
and the honorable guest would guide his ship
far away from there.
The brave one then requested Hrunting,
the sword of excellent iron given by Ecglaf's son,
and thanked him for it.
He said it was a sharp weapon in battle,
a friendly partner in war. He praised the blade
with honest words, for he was a courageous man.
Now the warriors were ready to depart,
armed and eager, while their host went to his rest.

63 The brave hero quickly went to the seat of honor and greeted
Hrothgar.

# BOOK XXVI

64   Beowulf spoke, son of Ecgtheow:
"We, the sailors, want to go
see Hygelac now. We've found
friends here; you've been kind.
If I can earn more of your love,
I'll keep fighting for you!
If enemies bother you,
I'll bring thousands of warriors,
brave heroes, to help you.
Hygelac, the Geats' leader,
will support me with words and actions.
He'll let me serve you,
fighting battles and lending strength.
If Hrethric, your son, comes to the Geats,
he'll find friends there.
Brave men should visit far-off lands."
Hrothgar answered him, saying:
"God has given you wise words!
You're young but wise, strong and cautious.

If anything happens to Hygelac,
and you survive battles or danger,
the Sea-Geats won't find a better leader,
a guard for their treasures and heroes,
than you."
Your kinsmen will now have a peaceful kingdom!
I am pleased with your cleverness,
Beowulf, my dear friend!
Because of you, the Geat and Spear-Dane people
will have peace between them and avoid war.
As long as I am king of this vast realm,
let our treasures be shared, and let heroes
exchange gifts of gold on the ocean's surface.
Let each boat carry symbols of love
over the rolling waves. I believe my people
are united in loyalty to both friends and enemies,
and they value honor in the old ways."
Then, in the hall, Hrothgar's son
gave Beowulf twelve treasures
and trusted him to bring them to his beloved people,
returning home safely and quickly.
The renowned king of the Scyldings kissed
his beloved warrior, and tears flowed
from his old eyes. Though he had experienced many hardships,
he held onto the hope of seeing Beowulf again,
and hearing his voice in the hall. Beowulf was so dear to him.
He tried to banish the wild waves of emotion in his chest,
but deep in his soul, a secret longing remained,
locked away in his mind, burning in his veins.
Then Beowulf walked happily across the grass,
grateful for his gold and gifts. His ship awaited him,
anchored on the sea. As they moved forward,
they praised Hrothgar's generous gift. He was truly a remarkable
lord,

blameless in every way, despite his old age.
It reaches everyone, his great power.

# BOOK XXVII

67  Now, the brave men approached the ocean.

They were strong and wore armor. The leader noticed

the return of the trustworthy earl. From the hill,

they saw no enemies and the leader called out a welcome to the Weder clan.

They marched towards the ship with shiny armor

and brought horses and treasure.

The ship was loaded with precious items and had a tall mast with gems from Hrothgar.

Beowulf gave a golden sword to the boat-guard as a gift.

They boarded the ship and sailed away from Daneland.

They set up a sail and the ship glided through the waves smoothly. Soon,

they saw the familiar cliffs of Geatland. They anchored the ship

and a guard waited for them on the shore.

He tied the ship tightly, so it wouldn't be taken away by the waves.

Beowulf ordered his men to bring the gold and jewels, as they didn't have to travel far to give them to the ring-giver.

68     Hygelac lived in a grand house by the close sea-wall, along with his clan.

The house was impressive, and the king was a heroic figure.

The hall stood tall, and Hygd, the young and wise daughter of Haereth, lived there.

Although she had only lived in the fortress for a few winters,

she was not modest in her ways.

She generously gave precious treasures to the Geatish men, unlike Thryth,

who was known for her pride and cruel actions.

No one dared to look directly at Thryth, except for her husband, as anyone else who tried would face certain death.

These deadly consequences were swift and harsh. Thryth's actions were not befitting of a queen,

even if she was unrivaled in beauty.

It was not right for a woman who should bring peace to harm

a dear warrior with anger and lies instead.

However, Hemming's relative intervened to stop her.

People also said that after Thryth married a noble young prince and went to his hall at her father's request,

she caused fewer horrors and acts of evil.

She thrived in her new role, living a rich and prosperous life as the faithful wife of a great warrior.

Offa, the prince she married, was highly praised as one of the greatest heroes that anyone had ever heard of,

known far and wide for his fighting skills and generosity.

69     The brave warrior Eomer was a wise ruler of his kingdom.

He had the support of his loyal heroes and was related to Hemming.

Eomer's grandfather was Garmund, known for his fierce skills in battle.

# BOOK XXVIII

 THE BRAVE ONE and his companions hurried along the sandy beach and the wide paths.

The sun, like a giant candle, shone from the south.

With strong steps, they walked to their destination, where the young king,

a slayer of enemies, lived within his fortress.

This king was known as the protector of heroes.

Beowulf's arrival was quickly reported to Hygelac, who ruled over the court.

The loyal warrior returned safely and full of life from his adventures.

The ruler made room for Beowulf as ordered and they sat together,

surrounded by family.

Hygelac warmly greeted Beowulf and asked him about his journey.

In the grand hall, Haereth's daughter came in, carrying a cup of wine for the heroes.

Hygelac was curious to know what Beowulf had accomplished during his time away.

He wanted to hear about Beowulf's battles
and if he had been able to help King Hrothgar with his problems.
Hygelac was worried about his dear friend, afraid that he might have faced danger.

He had advised Beowulf not to fight the fierce monster, Grendel,
and instead, let the South-Danes handle their own troubles.
Now, he thanked God for the safe return of Beowulf.
Beowulf said to Hygelac, the ruler:
"Many people know about the fierce battle
between Grendel and me, which took place
on the field where he caused much sorrow
for the Scyldings. I avenged their sufferings.
No one from Grendel's family
can boast about that fight at dawn,
against the most hated creature
that ever lived! But first, I went
to greet Hrothgar in the hall,
where the famous kinsman of Healfdene
assigned me a seat next to his son.
The warriors were lively and joyful;
I have never seen such merry men in a hall!
Then the noble queen, a peacemaker,
went through the hall and encouraged the young men,
giving them golden clasps before taking her own seat.
Hrothgar's daughter, Freawaru, often served
the ale-cup to the heroes one by one,
as I heard the companions call her.
She offered them adorned gold. She, a wealthy maiden, is promised
to the happy son of Froda.
Hrothgar, the protector of the kingdom, thinks it wise
to marry her thus and prevent any feud or bloodshed.

But sadly, when men are killed, the weapons
are not peaceful for long, even if the bride is beautiful!
The lord of the Heathobards will probably not be pleased.
Each of his loyal followers
when a warrior from the brave group of Danes
walks with the lady through their hall,
the ancient heirlooms shine brightly upon him,
covered with rings, treasures from the Heathobards,
and weapons once proudly wielded
until they were lost in battle,
cost both the loyal warrior and their lives.
Then, as they drink ale and gaze upon these heirlooms,
an old warrior, wise in the ways of war,
with a stern mood and heavy heart,
tests the young hero's spirit and strength
and stirs up hatred with words like these:
"Can't you see the sword
that your father carried into battle,
under his helmet, the most beloved of blades,
before the Danish people killed him
and took control of Withergild's position?
The heroes were slain, those brave Scyldings!
Now, the son of a bloodthirsty Dane,
proud of his treasure, walks in this hall,
delighting in killing, and carrying the jewel
that rightfully should belong to you!
He constantly provokes and urges him
with sharp words, until an opportunity comes
where Freawaru's warrior, because of his father's actions,
must sleep in eternal slumber due to a fatal blow,
losing his life, while the loyal warrior runs away,
knowing the land well.
And so, both sides break their oaths,
when Ingeld's heart fills with hatred for war

and love for his wife cools

after the troubled waves of conflict.

That's why I do not trust the faith of the Heathobards."

73 Because of the Danes and their love and peace agreement,

I won't dwell on that.

Instead, I'll talk about Grendel and how the battle unfolded.

When Grendel, a ferocious monster, came to attack us,

he found us guarding the hall. He killed Hondscio, a brave warrior,

by biting him and devouring him.

But Grendel didn't leave the hall empty-handed. He tried to grab me too,

but I fought back and he couldn't hurt me.

I fought back against Grendel and won, bringing honor to your people, my prince.

Grendel fled, but he left his hand behind in the hall.

He died in the ocean.

In return for my victory, the Danes rewarded me with gold and treasures.

74 We all sat down at the big table to eat.

The old king, who had been through a lot, told stories of the past.

Sometimes he played his harp and sang songs.

He would share tales of wonder

and also talk about his younger days.

His heart was filled with both joy and sadness as he remembered the passing of time.

We spent the whole day in the hall, eating and enjoying ourselves. When night fell,

Grendel's mother, seeking revenge for her son's death, attacked us.

She was a scary monster, and she killed one of our friends, Aeschere.

The next morning, we couldn't even give him a proper farewell.

Grendel's mother took his body and dumped it in a river.

This made King Hrothgar very sad.

He asked me to help and promised me a reward.

So, I agreed to go after Grendel's mother.

We fought underwater, and there was blood everywhere.

I bravely struck Grendel's mother with a strong sword,

cutting off her head and saving my own life.

It was a dangerous battle, but I survived.

However, my journey was not yet over.

The son of Healfdene, the great king, rewarded me with valuable gifts to show his gratitude.

# BOOK XXIX

76 THIS KING FOLLOWED old customs and made sure I was well rewarded for my strength and bravery.

Healfdene's heir, the leader of the heroes, gave me valuable gifts that I can now offer to you, my prince.

Your kindness is the only thing that can make me happy.

I don't have many family members, just you, Hygelac!

Then Beowulf had his soldiers bring him a special flag with a boar head on it, a tall battle helmet, and a gray breastplate.

He said, "The wise old king, Hrothgar, gave me this armor and told me to tell you its story.

It was once owned by Heorogar, the king before him,

but he didn't pass it on to his son, Heoroweard, who he loved dearly.

Take good care of it!"

I also heard that he gave the king four strong horses and special weapons.

This is how family should treat each other, not with tricks or betrayal.

Hygelac always loved his nephew and took care of him.

He also gave a beautiful necklace to Hygd, the king's daughter, and three horses.

Everyone could see how much she loved wearing that necklace.

This is the story of Ecgtheow's son, and it shows what a great family he came from.

He was a man known for great deeds
and honorable acts. He never harmed
a friend or family member. He was not cruel,
despite his great strength, a gift from God.
For a long time, he was rejected
and viewed as worthless by the Geatish warriors.
The leader of the mead hall often failed
to show him any favor.
The strong men thought he was lazy and useless,
a prince of no value. But eventually,
the honored warrior received his reward for all his troubles.
Then the great earl commanded to bring in
the precious heirloom of Hrethel, the brave chieftain,
adorned with gold. No Geat had ever seen
a more magnificent sword.
He placed the sword in Beowulf's lap
and gave him seven thousand furs,
along with a house and high seat. They shared
the land and inheritance by bloodline,
but the king was held in higher regard
because he ruled over the entire kingdom.
As the years went by,
tragedy struck as Hygelac and his successor, Heardred, died
in a battle under the shield-wall,
killed by the fierce warriors of the Heatho-Scilfings,
who sought revenge for Hereric's death.
Then Beowulf became the king of this vast land
and ruled it wisely for fifty winters.
He was a respected and experienced ruler,

protecting his land until one night,

a dragon awoke in darkness,

one who guarded a treasure hoard inside a steep hill.

A narrow path led to it,

No one knew about the hidden cave.

But one day, a man stumbled upon it by chance.

He found a shiny golden goblet

and decided to keep it, sneaking away while the dragon was asleep.

Little did he know, this would anger the dragon,

and the consequences would be severe for both the man and his people.

# BOOK XXX



HE WENT that way without wanting to,
in great danger of losing his life, to the dragon's treasure,
compelled by a prince's servant.
Out of fear, he ran away from the deadly monster and sought shelter in the cave.
The sight of the dragon's hoard terrified him,
but quickly he gathered his courage and took a cup from the treasure.
There were many other ancient heirlooms hidden there as well,
left behind by forgotten earls from long ago.
The last surviving member of his noble family chose to protect the treasure,
even though his time was short.
Nearby, by the cliff and the sea, a new burial mound stood,
where he laid his precious possessions and his piled-up gold.
He spoke few words, entrusting the earth to guard what noble men once owned.
Sadly, all his kinsmen had been killed in battle,

leaving him alone without anyone to wield a sword or to clean
the valuable cup.

The helmet, adorned with gold, would lose its shine

as there were no polishers left to make it bright and glorious.

The brave warriors who used to fight fearlessly,

their armor now rusty and forgotten,

cannot protect themselves anymore.

No more beautiful harp music,

no joyful cheers in the woods!

The hall is quiet without the sound

of horses racing in the town.

My family and friends,

the best of our people, have been taken away by battle and
death."

He mourned and wept, feeling very sad all alone.

His sorrow never left him, day or night,

until death finally came.

The evil dragon discovered his hidden treasure,

a dragon who breathes fire and terrorizes the land at night.

This dragon guards the ancient graves and stolen gold for many
years,

but he doesn't truly gain anything from it.

This dragon had kept the treasure hidden under the earth

for three hundred winters until one day,

someone stirred up anger inside him.

They took a valuable cup from the treasure,

pleading for peace with the dragon.

The thief was granted their request,

and the ruler saw ancient treasures for the first time.

When the dragon woke up, he noticed something was missing.

He found the footprint of the thief,

who had secretly taken something near the dragon's head.

If only he had the grace of The Wielder,

he could escape from these troubles and find a safe place to live.

That guardian of gold was content no more.
He searched anxiously over the ground,
eager to find the person who had wronged him in his sleep.
With savage fury, he circled the burial mound,
but found nobody there, no one in sight...
However, he still desired war,
craving a battle. He entered the mound,
looking for the cup, and soon discovered
that someone had stolen his treasure,
his precious gold. The guardian waited
impatiently until evening came;
filled with anger, he wanted to retaliate
by setting everything on fire for the loss of the cup.
Now the day had passed
just as the dragon had hoped. It no longer wanted
to remain near the mound, but instead, it soared
engulfed in flames: a terrifying sight
for the people; and soon, it brought
a terrible end to their lord's fate.

# BOOK XXXI

 Then the evil dragon spewed fire and set homes ablaze.

The flames spread, terrifying all the people.

No one was safe from the menacing creature as it flew overhead.

The dragon's destructive fury could be seen far and wide,

causing fear and hatred among the Geatish people.

At dawn, the dragon retreated to its hidden lair and cherished hoard.

It had engulfed the land in flames, leaving nothing but destruction in its wake.

The dragon believed its barrow to be unbreakable, a false sense of security.

Quickly and truthfully, Beowulf was told of the devastation
that befell his cherished home, the finest in the land.

This news brought immense sorrow to the wise old king,
who assumed he had angered his mighty God
and brought divine punishment upon his people.

In his troubled heart, dark thoughts swirled, which was rare for him.

The dragon had ravaged their fortress and sunk it in the waves.

But the valiant king, leader of the Weders, planned his revenge.

He commanded his loyal warriors to craft a remarkable shield made of iron,

fully aware that wooden shields would be useless against fire.

This noble prince was destined to confront the dragon and end his own fleeting life

upon this earth, along with the creature that had guarded the hoard for so long.

He considered it a disgrace as a ring-giver to chase after the flying foe with an army.

He was not afraid of the wide-ranging battle,
nor did he fear the dragon's strength and courage.
He had faced many daring adventures
and war challenges since he proudly conquered
Hrothgar's hall and defeated Grendel's kin,
the vile monsters! One of the most memorable
was the hand-to-hand fight where Hygelac fell,
the ruler of Geats, while battling in the Frisian land.
Hygelac, the son of Hrethel, died by sword wounds,
overwhelmed by enemy blades. Beowulf escaped
by his own strength and swimming ability,
even though he was alone and burdened with
thirty suits of armor when he reached the sea!
The boastful Hetwaras could not match
Beowulf's skill in combat, as they brought
their shields to the fight. Only a few managed
to survive the encounter with the hero and return home!
Then Ecgtheow's son swam across the ocean,
feeling lonely and sorrowful, seeking his homeland,
where Hygd offered him treasures and a kingdom,
ignoring her son's strength to defend their land
from enemy invaders after Hygelac's death.
The grieving ones could not, at that moment,
consider making the young Heardred their ruler,

as Beowulf supported him with encouraging words
and bestowed honor upon him until he grew older
and became the leader of the Weder-Geats.
Wandering exiles, the sons of Ohtere, sought him
across the seas.
He was a strong and brave warrior who refused to yield
to the Scylfings' rule, the mighty and powerful enemy.
He fought against them in the land of Sweden,
showing his courage and strength. This led to the downfall
of Heardred, the king who offered him shelter.
Unfortunately, Heardred was killed in battle,
a victim of a deadly sword strike, the cruel blow.
But Beowulf, the son of Ongentheow, returned
to his own home and land after Heardred's death.
Now, Beowulf became the new ruler of the Geats,
a great and wise king who took charge of the kingdom's throne.

# BOOK XXXII

 In the days that followed his lord's fall,

he wanted to avenge him.

He became a friend to Eadgils, who had no one else to turn to.

He sent warriors and weapons across the sea to Ohtere's son,

to repay him for the cruel deeds done to his own people.

The son of Ecgtheow had faced many dangers and performed brave deeds,

until this day arrived and he had to face the dragon.

With eleven comrades filled with anger, the Geat lord went to find the dragon.

He knew who had caused all the harm and killed his kinsmen.

The king had received a precious cup as a reward,

but it sparked conflict and troubles.

A captive, burdened with worries,

led them reluctantly to the cave that was near the ocean's waves.

It was full of treasure--gold and jewels.

A fierce guardian protected the treasures, hiding in the cave.

It was not easy for anyone to go inside.

The hero king sat on the headland and greeted his companions.

His soul was heavy, torn between life and death.

Death was close, ready to take the old man's soul

and separate it from his body.

Beowulf, the son of Ecgtheow, spoke and said, "I have faced many struggles in my youth."

I remember all the mighty feuds from my youth.

When I was seven years old, the king,

a friend to his people, took me from my father,

he cared for and raised me, King Hrethel,

with food and support, loyal as family.

While I lived there, he never treated me worse

than his own sons, Herebeald and Haethcyn and my brother Hygelac.

But, by a terrible accident, the oldest of them,

through a tragic mistake, brought death upon himself.

Haethcyn killed him with a stray arrow,

accidentally striking his dear lord,

one brother killing another with a deadly shot.

An unforgivable fight, a terrible sin,

a horror for Hrethel; yet, as difficult as it was,

the prince's death stayed unavenged!

It's too heartbreaking for an old man

to witness his young child hanging from the gallows.

He composes a sorrowful poem,

a song of grief for his son hanging there,

like a feast for ravens; no rescue now

can come from the old, weak man!

As morning breaks, he still thinks of the heir

who is gone elsewhere; he doesn't expect

to live long enough to see his city

guarding his wealth, now that one son

has met the fate that his actions brought upon him.

He looks sadly at his son's empty abode,

a deserted wine-hall with cold, empty rooms
where joyful celebrations used to take place.

# BOOK XXXIII

87    THEN HE GOES to his room and sings a sad song
        about his lost loved one. The house and everything in it
        feel too big and empty.
        The king, who was supposed to protect Herebeald,
        is filled with sadness.
        He couldn't find a way to seek revenge for the terrible crime
        that was committed. He couldn't even confront the person who
did it
        because he didn't want to cause more harm.
        Because of his sorrow, he gave up his own happiness and chose
to live in darkness.
        When the king passed away, he left his lands and cities to his
sons,
        as wealthy people usually do.
        But there was a fight between the Swedes and Geats over the sea.
        It was a terrible battle that happened
        when Hrethel died and Ongentheow's children wanted to keep
fighting
        instead of making peace over the waters.

They pushed their armies to attack each other near Hreosnabeorh.

The people of my tribe sought revenge for that feud,

and it's known by many that there was a lot of sad fighting.

One of our own died in that battle,

Haethcyn, who was the first of the Geats.

In the morning, I heard that Haethcyn's killer, Eofor,

fought and killed the murderer with a sword. The battle was fierce,

and Ongentheow, the old leader of the Swedes, fell.

Eofor was determined and did not hesitate to deliver a deadly blow.

"For all that Hrethel did for me, I repaid him by using my powerful sword in battle.

He entrusted me with land, a home, and a house.

He didn't need help from the Swedes or the Spear-Danes."

or from men of the Gifths, to get him help,

someone worse warrior to buy with payment!

I always fought in the front, leading the way,

and I will continue to fight as long as I live

with this trusty blade, which has proven faithful

since the day Daeghrefn, the Hugas' champion,

fell by my hand. He did not return

to the Frisian king with the spoils and treasures,

but in the struggle, he, the brave nobleman,

fell. He was not killed by a sword,

but his bones were broken by a powerful grip,

and his life was taken. Now, this sword's edge,

hard and sharp, will contend for the treasure, with my hand."

Beowulf spoke and made a battle vow,

his final one: "I have survived many wars in my youth.

Now, once more, old defender of the people, I will seek a feud,

and perform mighty deeds, if the dark destroyer

comes out of his cave to fight me!"

Then, Beowulf greeted his helmeted heroes,
his loyal comrades in war, for the last time,
saying: "I would not bring a weapon,
nor a sword to fight the serpent, if only I knew
how to win against such an enemy,
like I did in the fight against Grendel.
But now, I must fear fire and poisonous breath,
so I bring a breastplate and shield with me.
I will not retreat even a step from the guardian of the mound.
One battle will end our war by the wall,
as fate decides, the master of all mankind.
I am brave in spirit, but I won't boast about defeating this flying
creature."

89 Now, warriors clad in armor, stay near the burial mound.

Let us see who will fare better in battle. Wait here and watch.

This fight is only meant for me to face the monster and be the
hero. I will win the treasure or death will take your king and lord!

The brave champion stood up, holding his shield, relying on his
own strength.

He wore his armor proudly under the cliffs.

He didn't take the path of a coward!

Soon he saw an arch of stone near the wall,
and inside, a stream flowing out of the burial mound.

The water was hot with fire.

He knew he couldn't approach the treasure safely
or endure the deep water because of the dragon's flames.

Filled with rage, the warrior prince of the Geats
shouted loudly beneath the gray rocks.

The dragon, the guardian of the treasure, heard a human voice
and became even more furious.

There was no more peace!

The dragon unleashed its poisonous breath from the cave
and the noise echoed through the rocks.

The Geatish lord raised his shield, standing strong by the stone path,

facing the loathed creature.

The serpent, with its coils, approached, ready for a fight.

he brave king drew his sharp sword,

The two warriors were filled with fear as they faced their formidable foe.

The brave king stood boldly with his shield held high,

ready to defend himself.

The blazing serpent swiftly approached, spiraling forward with speed and agility.

The shield protected the king's body for a short time,

but not as long as he had hoped. Fate denied him

the much-needed moment of respite and the chance to claim victory.

With all his might, the lord of the Geats swung his inherited weapon

to strike the fierce creature.

However, the blade's edge was dulled and failed

to penetrate the dragon's tough hide as strongly as the noble king had intended.

The keeper of the burial mound became enraged by the powerful blow.

He unleashed deadly flames that spread far and wide,

leaving no room for the Geats' lord to boast about his triumph.

His trusted sword had failed him in battle, leaving him defenseless and vulnerable.

The path that the respected heir of Ecgtheow had to walk towards his foe

was not an easy one.

He had no choice but to find a new home far away,

like all men must eventually leave this life behind.

It did not take long for the fierce champions to engage in battle once again.

The keeper of the hoard was encouraged by his renewed strength
and pressed the folk-commander by engulfing him in flames.
Without the support of his comrades,
who had retreated into the woods, the lord of the Geats faced
great danger.
They risked their lives to save others.
But one person's heart was troubled.
True kinship can never be damaged in a noble heart.

# BOOK XXXIV

92 His name was Wiglaf, the son of Weohstan.

He was a brave warrior and a loyal follower of his lord,

the leader of the Scylfings, Aelfhere.

When he saw his king in trouble, he remembered the gifts and honors

his king had given him. Without hesitation,

he grabbed his shield and drew his old sword, a precious heirloom.

This sword had once belonged to Eanmund,

who was killed in battle by Weohstan.

It was given to Weohstan by Onela, the king of the Eotens.

Wiglaf wore his father's armor and kept it safe until he was old enough to earn his place as a warrior.

Now, he was ready to fight alongside his lord for the first time.

Wiglaf knew that his soul and his loyalty would not waver in battle.

So when the dragon attacked, Wiglaf stood tall and brave.

He spoke words of wisdom to his comrades,

reminding them of the promise they made to their king,

to fight by his side no matter what.

93 We were chosen by our noble master,
selected from his army to stand by his side.
He honored us with treasures, swords and helmets,
because he believed in our strength and bravery.
He hoped to complete this heroic task alone,
defending our people and earning greater glory.
But now the day has come when our leader needs us,
when he needs the might of brave warriors.
Let us join him in this fiery battle,
supporting our hero while the danger is near.
I swear, God is my witness,
I would rather burn with my lord
than carry our shields home without a fight.
It would be a shame if only the king
among the Geatish warriors suffered and fell.
My sword, helmet, breastplate, and shield
will serve us both in this fight.
With a determination fueled by the smell of blood,
I stride forward to aid my leader,
my battle-helmet shining, and I speak these words:
"Beloved Beowulf, be brave and strong,
just as you vowed in your youthful days
to never let your glory fade.
Now, in your great deeds,
you stand firm, mighty prince.
Protect your life, and I will stand with you."
As I spoke, the dragon approached once more,
a monstrous creature filled with rage,
spewing flames in search of its enemies.

94 The evil men were hated.
The heat from the dragon's flames burned Beowulf's shield,
and his breastplate did not protect him from the spear.

But quickly, he went under his kinsman's shield, since his own was burned.

The brave king still had his glory in mind.

With all his might, he thrust his sword into the dragon's head fueled by his hatred. But his sword, Naegling, broke in the battle.

His old, gray sword was no match for the dragon.

No iron edge could help him in this fight.

Beowulf was too strong and struck too hard.

None of the sturdy swords he wielded were of any use.

Then, for the third time, the dragon attacked the hero.

It rushed toward him, fierce and fiery.

Its sharp teeth closed around his neck, and his blood poured from his chest.

# BOOK XXXV

95 IN HIS TIME OF NEED, the brave earl displayed his noble qualities
of skill, sharpness, and enduring courage.
Despite being burned, he fearlessly assisted his kinsman
by striking the repulsive beast with his sword,
piercing its bright and polished scales, causing its fire to weaken
and fade.
Regaining his composure, the king reached for his trusty war-knife
hanging by his chestplate and, with a powerful blow, cleaved the
serpent in two,
ending its life.
They had both vanquished the foe, these two noble warriors,
as true earls should in times of danger!
This would be the final act of victory for the king,
marking the end of his legendary deeds in the world.
But with this triumph came a new wound, inflicted by the
dragon,
causing a searing and deep pain as poison spread through his
body.

Wise in his thoughts, the prince made his way to a towering rocky wall, where he sat

and gazed upon the magnificent structure built by giants,

its stone arches and sturdy columns supporting the earthly hall for eternity.

However, the unparalleled attendant had a task to perform--

to tend to his beloved and blood-covered lord, the victorious and weary king,

by removing his helmet and washing his wounds with water.

In spite of his injury, Beowulf spoke, aware that his time for earthly happiness

had come to an end

and the remaining days of his life had fled.

Death was near, and he said, "I would like to give my weapons, my arm, to any blood of mine"



If anyone were to inherit my war gear after I pass,

may it be a worthy descendant of my own bloodline.

I have ruled over this people for fifty years.

There was not a single king from the neighboring clans

who dared to wage war against me or threaten me with terror.

I stayed at home, accepting whatever fate came my way,

and I took care of my own.

I never sought out conflicts or made false promises or oaths.

Despite being fatally wounded, I am content with all these things.

I will not face the wrath of the Ruler-of-Man when my life must come to an end,

even though I have killed kinsmen in battle.

Now, quickly go and see the treasure hoard beneath the ancient rock, which Wiglaf treasures.

The serpent lies defeated, sleeping and heartbroken without its stolen treasure.

Hurry back. I long to see the beautiful heirlooms,

the golden treasures and precious gems.

I want to find joy in their sight before I peacefully surrender my life

and the rule that I have held for so long."

# BOOK XXXVI

 Once upon a time, the son of Weohstan swiftly followed his wounded king's orders.

He went to the place where the king's enemies were defeated and found a lot of treasures.

There were gold and jewels everywhere!

He saw old rusty helmets, ancient arm rings, and valuable bowls.

There was also a beautifully crafted gold banner.

The dragon was gone, killed by the hero's sword.

The hero took many gold beakers and plates and grabbed the banner.

He realized that his king, the lord of the Weders, might still be alive.

So, he hurried back, eager to find out.

 He grew weaker near the cave wall.

So he carried the load. He found his wounded lord and king
close to death. The loyal warrior
splashed water on him until he could speak.

Beowulf spoke, wise and sad, looking at the gold.

"I thank God and the Wonder-maker

for this treasure I see, to the Lord of Heaven,
for the grace to give such gifts to my people
before the day I die!
Now I have traded my life for this treasure,
so take care of my land! I won't stay any longer.
Build a burial mound for my ashes
by the shore, on the high Hrones Headland,
so travelers on the ocean can see
Beowulf's Barrow when they sail by."
He removed his gold necklace from his neck,
the brave king, and gave it to his vassal,
along with a shiny gold helmet, breastplate, and ring,
for the young warrior to use with joy.
"You are the last one left of our people,
the only one with the Waegmunding name.
Fate has taken them all,
my noble line, to the land of death.
Now it is my turn to follow them."
These were the final words the wise old man
held in his heart before the fires of death
embraced him. His soul fled from his chest
to seek the rewards of the saints.

# BOOK XXXVII

 ONCE UPON A TIME, there was a young hero who had a very sad moment.

He found his beloved lord lying on the ground, not breathing anymore.

Nearby, the mighty dragon that had taken his lord's life also lay defeated,

unable to guard its treasure.

Its sharp teeth and strong claws were useless against the hero's weapons.

The dragon had fallen to the ground, injured and weak,

no longer able to fly or boast of its treasures.

It was the hero, the king, who had defeated the dragon.

Not many people are brave enough to face a deadly dragon and enter its lair.

But the hero, Beowulf, risked it all for the chance to protect his people.

Unfortunately, he paid a great price for that bravery.

He lost his life while battling the dragon.

And the dragon, too, met its end in that fight.

After the battle, some of the cowardly warriors who had abandoned their king returned to the scene.

They felt ashamed of their fear and carried their shields and
armor.

They looked at Wiglaf, the loyal warrior who had stayed with the
king until the end.

He tried to wake the king with water, but it was too late.

The king had passed away,

and there was nothing Wiglaf could do to bring him back.

Wiglaf was filled with sorrow and he spoke to the other warriors,

reminding them of the gifts and rewards their lord had given
them.

He had given them gold rings and armor to protect them.

But these warriors had failed to stand up for their lord

when the enemy attacked.

The hero had to face the enemy alone, with only his sword to
defend himself.

Wiglaf pointed out the consequences of their cowardice.

Their lord's death meant that they would lose their homes and
land,

and they would be known throughout the land as failures.

He believed that death was better than living with shame and
dishonor.

This was a hard truth to hear, but it was an important lesson for
the warriors to learn.

They had failed their lord, and now they must face the consequences of their actions.

# BOOK XXXVIII

101 THE MESSENGERS WERE SENT to announce the outcome of the battle at the fort on the cliff.

The brave warriors on the morning ride were filled with sorrow and uncertainty.

Would they welcome their beloved lord home, or would they mourn his death?

The herald didn't hold back any news as he rode up the headland.

"Now, the generous leader of the people of Weder lies on his deathbed.

The Lord of Geats sleeps by the serpent's attack!

Next to him is the killer, wounded by the knife,

but no sword could hurt the terrible creature.

Wiglaf, Weohstan's son, sits beside Beowulf, a living warrior with a heavy heart,

guarding both friend and foe.

Now our people can prepare for war, as the fall of the king is known to the Frisians

and the Franks far and wide."

"The conflict began when Hygelac, our king, fell in battle
against the Hugas and sailed with his fleet to Frisian land.
The Hetwaras defeated him with their great strength and he died fighting.
He couldn't give any treasure to his friends!
And ever since then, the Merowings have abandoned us.
We can't expect peace or loyalty from the Swedish people.
It's widely known how Ongentheow, at Ravenswood,
took Haethcyn Hrethling's hope and life when the Geats ventured into battle
against the Warlike-Scylfings."
The old and wise Ohtere's father fought back,
he killed the sea king and saved his wife,
his good wife who was robbed of her gold,
she was Ohtere and Onela's mother.
Then he chased his enemies, who ran away,
hurting and searching for safety,
they went to Ravenswood without their leader.
He besieged them there, the ones that were left,
the tired and wounded, threatening them with more pain,
throughout the night, he warned that some
would be killed by his sword the next day,
and others would hang from a tree
for the ravens to feast on. But then, at dawn
those desperate men were saved
when they heard King Hygelac's horn,
the sound of his trumpet; the loyal king
had followed their footsteps with his faithful group.

# BOOK XXXIX

103 THE SWEDES and Geats were fighting,
there was a big battle between them.
The old king and his loyal followers
went to his castle, feeling sad:
Ongentheow, the earl, went to his fort.
He had already tested Hygelac's bravery,
he knew that Hygelac was strong,
so he didn't want to fight them anymore,
he didn't hope to save his treasures,
his child, and his wife. So he returned
to his castle, old and tired. But then,
Hygelac's army came with a lot of fighting,
they marched proudly across the peaceful fields
until they reached the fortified town.
Ongentheow, the old man with a long beard,
had to defend himself with his sword,
the people's king was trapped
and Eofor was angry at him.
Wulf, the son of Wonred, struck

the king with his weapon and blood flowed
from the king's head. The old Scylfing
wasn't afraid, he fought back
and hit his enemy harder.
But Wonred's son was too slow
to defend himself from the old king,
the king hit him on the head with his helmet.
The young warrior fell down to the ground,
but he wasn't dead yet, although he was hurt.
Then one of Hygelac's brave soldiers
killed the old king with a big sword,
the sword went through the king's helmet
and broke through the shield. The king sank down.
The herdsman, who was a loyal member of his people,
was gravely wounded.

Many rushed to tend to his wounds and carry him to safety as quickly as possible.

Eofor seized Ongentheow's armor--
his breastplate, sword, and helmet--
and brought them to Hygelac. Hygelac gratefully accepted the treasures

and promised Eofor and Wulf a great reward, which he later fulfilled.

When Hygelac returned home, he rewarded Eofor and Wulf with land and precious rings,
an incredibly valuable gift.

He even gave his daughter in marriage to Eofor as a sign of his gratitude.

This feud and the hatred between enemies
are the reasons why we believe that the Swedes will seek revenge
for the death of their comrades, the warriors from the Scylfing tribe.

Once they learn that our leader, who always protected our land and treasures, has fallen,

they will surely come after us.
Now we must hasten and pay our respects to our Geatish lord
by taking him to his final resting place.
We will burn his body on a funeral pyre,
along with all the valuable and precious items he acquired in his
lifetime.
No one should keep any of those treasures,
as they will all be consumed by the fire.
But she will not wear fancy jewelry,
Instead she is sad and has lost her gold.
She will often have to wander alone,
Now that our lord is no longer happy,
No longer joyful. Many cold mornings
They will hold their spears tightly,
Raised up high; and no one will play the harp
To bring them joy; only the pale raven,
Glad over the fallen, will praise his feast
And brag to the eagle how bravely he ate
When he and the wolf devoured the dead."
So he shared his sad news,
And he spoke the truth, the loyal man,
With his words and actions. The warriors stood up;
Sad and tearful, they climbed the Cliff-of-Eagles,
And went to see the amazing sight.
On the beach, they found
Their lifeless lord, who had given them many rings in the past.
This was the end of his brave days; death had taken
The mighty king of the Weders in a terrible battle.
There, they also saw a strange creature,
Disgusting and lying near their leader,
Lifeless on the ground. It was a fiery dragon,
A scary monster, burned by flames.
If they measured it in feet, it was fifty long.
It used to fly high in the sky at night,

And return to its den; but now, in death's grip,

It had come to the end of its happy life in the earth-hall.

Next to it, there were cups and jars;

Dishes and swords, once beautiful,

Now covered in rust, as they rested on the ground,

Waiting there for a thousand winters.

All of that precious treasure, that gold

From long ago, was under a powerful spell.

106  The treasure-hall was off-limits to everyone,

except for God, the King of Heaven,

who could choose to grant someone

the ability to unlock the hoard,

but only if they were worthy in His eyes.

# BOOK XL

107 It was a dangerous path that he walked on,

hiding inside the hall with his secret treasure beneath the wall

The guardian of the hall had killed one of his enemies and sought revenge.

It's amazing how a brave and mighty man often meets his end,

no longer able to live in the hall with his loved ones.

Beowulf, when he entered the barrow and faced the guardian,

didn't know how he would leave this world.

The princes who had hidden the gold had cursed it, so anyone who dared to take it

would be plagued with horror and suffer in hell.

But Beowulf wasn't motivated by greed for gold, he was guided by the grace of heaven.

Wiglaf, son of Weohstan, spoke up,

saying that often many warriors must suffer because of one person's decisions,

just like they were suffering now.

The king didn't listen to their advice to leave the gold guardian alone

and let him lie where he belonged, waiting for the end of the
world.

This treasure was now theirs but it came at a great cost, with
their king meeting a grim fate.

Wiglaf admitted that he had gone inside the hall and seen the
treasure,

taking what he could carry and bringing it back hastily.
To my ruler and lord. He was still alive,
his mind still sharp. The wise old man
spoke many words of sorrow and sent his greetings.
He asked that when he passed away,
you build a tall mound on his funeral pyre,
a great memorial. He was the greatest warrior
in all the world, while he enjoyed his jewels and kingdom.
Now, let's quickly go a second time
to see and explore this hidden treasure,
these marvelous walls, following the path I'll show you.
Once we gather near, you can marvel
at the broad gold and rings. Prepare the stretcher
that we'll use to carry out our king and leader,
the beloved man who will rest there for a long time,
safe in the care of the great God."
Then the son of Weohstan, a brave chief,
commanded many heroes
who owned homes in this land to bring
firewood from distant places for the famous warrior's funeral.
"The fire will consume him,
and the flames will feed on the fearless warrior
who stood strong in the rain of iron,
when a storm of arrows flew from the enemy,
shooting over the shield-wall. Arrows stuck firm,
well-fletched with feathers, following the point."
And now, the wise young son of Weohstan
chose seven of the bravest warriors,

the best he found among the group,
and went with these warriors, a group of eight,
to the enemy's home. One of them held
a lit torch and led the way.
They didn't need to draw lots to guard the treasure
once the warriors saw it in the hall.
They found the treasure, but there was no one guarding it.
They quickly took the precious items without feeling sad.
They threw the dragon into the water where it was swallowed by
the waves.
Then they loaded the gold onto a wagon and carried the king to
Hrones-Ness.

# BOOK XLI

 THE GEATS MADE a big fire on the ground for the funeral.

They put their leader's things on it, like helmets and armor.

Then they put their leader in the fire, and the heroes were sad.

The fire was very big and black smoke covered the sky. The wind was quiet.

The fire burned the leader's body until only bones were left.

The heroes were very sad. The old widow cried and was worried about what would happen next.

She thought there would be more deaths and battles and shame.

The smoke disappeared into the sky.

The Geats built a big hill by the ocean where people could see it.

It took them ten days to build it.

They made a wall around the hill with pieces of the pyre.

They put all the valuable things they took from the cave inside the hill.

People used to think the gold was important, but now it was just sitting there in the ground.

Then twelve brave warriors rode around the hill to honor their leader

and sing sad songs.
They praised their leader for his bravery and greatness,
which everyone knew and admired.
It's important to honor and love our friends,
especially when they pass away.
The people of Geatland mourned deeply
for their hero's departure.
They believed he was the best king among all,
loved and respected by everyone.